10/10

D0900298

STAR WARS®

EPISODE VI
RETURN OF THE JEDI™

VOLUME THREE

Script
ARCHIE GOODWIN

Art
AL WILLIAMSON
CARLOS GARZÓN

Colors
CARY PORTER
PERRY McNAMEE

Lettering
ED KING

Cover Art
AL WILLIAMSON

DARK HORSE COMICS

Spotlight

VISIT US AT
www.abdopublishing.com

Reinforced library bound edition published in 2010 by Spotlight, a division of the ABDO Group, 800 West 78th Street, Edina, Minnesota 55439. Spotlight produces high-quality reinforced library bound editions for schools and libraries. Published by agreement with Dark Horse Comics, Inc., and Lucasfilm Ltd.

Printed in the United States of America, Melrose Park, Illinois.
092009
012010

 PRINTED ON RECYCLED PAPER

Library of Congress Cataloging-in-Publication Data

Goodwin, Archie.
  Episode VI : return of the Jedi / based on the screenplay by George Lucas ; script adaptation Archie Goodwin ; artists Al Williamson & Carlos Garzon ; letterer Ed King. -- Reinforced library bound ed.
     p. cm. -- (Star wars)
  "Dark Horse Comics."
  ISBN 978-1-59961-705-3 (vol. 1) -- ISBN 978-1-59961-706-0 (vol. 2) -- ISBN 978-1-59961-707-7 (vol. 3) -- ISBN 978-1-59961-708-4 (vol. 4)
  1. Graphic novels. [1. Graphic novels.] I. Lucas, George, 1944- II. Williamson, Al, 1931- III. Garzon, Carlos. IV. Return of the Jedi (Motion picture) V. Title. VI. Title: Episode six. VII. Title: Return of the Jedi.
  PZ7.7.G656Epk 2010
  [Fic]--dc22
                                        2009030862

All Spotlight books have reinforced library bindings and are manufactured in the United States of America.

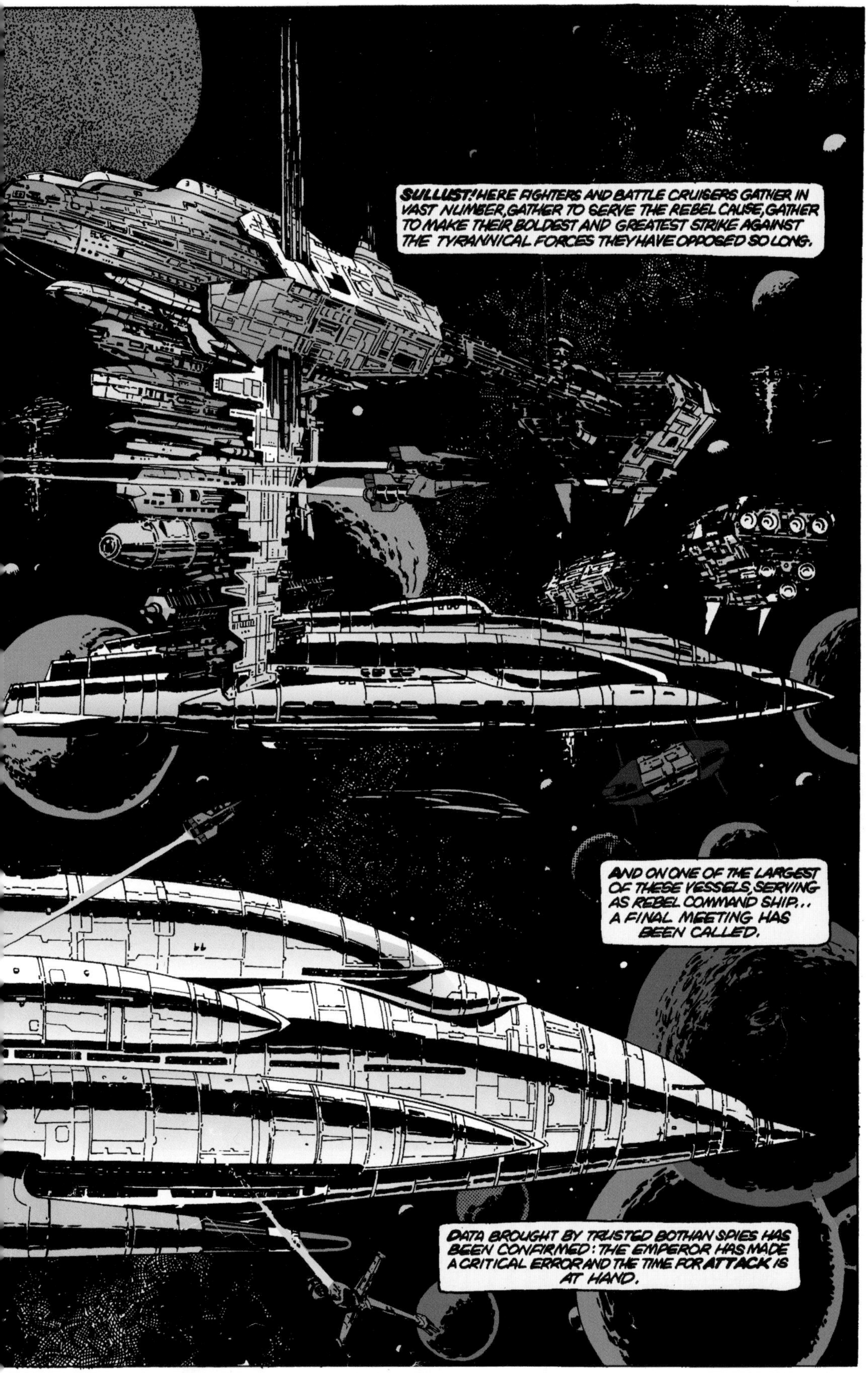
SULLUST! HERE FIGHTERS AND BATTLE CRUISERS GATHER IN VAST NUMBER, GATHER TO SERVE THE REBEL CAUSE, GATHER TO MAKE THEIR BOLDEST AND GREATEST STRIKE AGAINST THE TYRANNICAL FORCES THEY HAVE OPPOSED SO LONG.
AND ON ONE OF THE LARGEST OF THESE VESSELS, SERVING AS REBEL COMMAND SHIP... A FINAL MEETING HAS BEEN CALLED.
DATA BROUGHT BY TRUSTED BOTHAN SPIES HAS BEEN CONFIRMED: THE EMPEROR HAS MADE A CRITICAL ERROR AND THE TIME FOR ATTACK IS AT HAND.

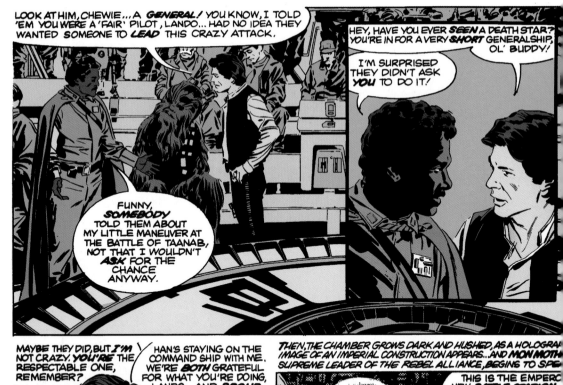

LOOK AT HIM, CHEWIE... A **GENERAL!** YOU KNOW, I TOLD 'EM YOU WERE A 'FAIR' PILOT, LANDO... HAD NO IDEA THEY WANTED SOMEONE TO **LEAD** THIS CRAZY ATTACK.

HEY, HAVE YOU EVER **SEEN** A DEATH STAR? YOU'RE IN FOR A VERY **SHORT** GENERALSHIP, OL' BUDDY!

I'M SURPRISED THEY DIDN'T ASK **YOU** TO DO IT!

FUNNY, **SOMEBODY** TOLD THEM ABOUT MY LITTLE MANEUVER AT THE BATTLE OF TAANAB, NOT THAT I WOULDN'T **ASK** FOR THE CHANCE ANYWAY.

MAYBE THEY DID, BUT **I'M** NOT CRAZY. **YOU'RE** THE RESPECTABLE ONE, REMEMBER?

HAN'S STAYING ON THE COMMAND SHIP WITH ME. WE'RE **BOTH** GRATEFUL FOR WHAT YOU'RE DOING, LANDO... AND **PROUD.**

THEN, THE CHAMBER GROWS DARK AND HUSHED, AS A HOLOGRAM IMAGE OF AN IMPERIAL CONSTRUCTION APPEARS... AND MON MOTHMA SUPREME LEADER OF THE REBEL ALLIANCE, BEGINS TO SPEAK.

THIS IS THE EMPEROR'S NEW **BATTLE STATION..** WEAPONS SYSTEMS ARE NOT YET **OPERATIONAL.** WITH THE IMPERIAL FLEET SPREAD THROUGHOUT THE GALAXY, VAINLY ATTEMPTING TO **ENGAGE** US...

IT IS RELATIVELY **UNPROTECTED.** MOST IMPORTANT, OUR SPY NETWORK HAS LEARNED THE **EMPEROR** IS PERSONALLY **OVERSEEING** THE CONSTRUCTION.

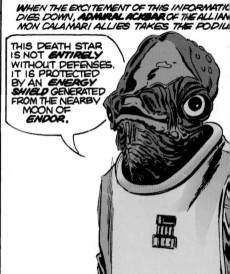

WHEN THE EXCITEMENT OF THIS INFORMATION DIES DOWN, **ADMIRAL ACKBAR** OF THE ALLIANCE'S MON CALAMARI ALLIES TAKES THE PODIUM.

THIS DEATH STAR IS NOT **ENTIRELY** WITHOUT DEFENSES. IT IS PROTECTED BY AN **ENERGY SHIELD** GENERATED FROM THE NEARBY MOON OF **ENDOR.**

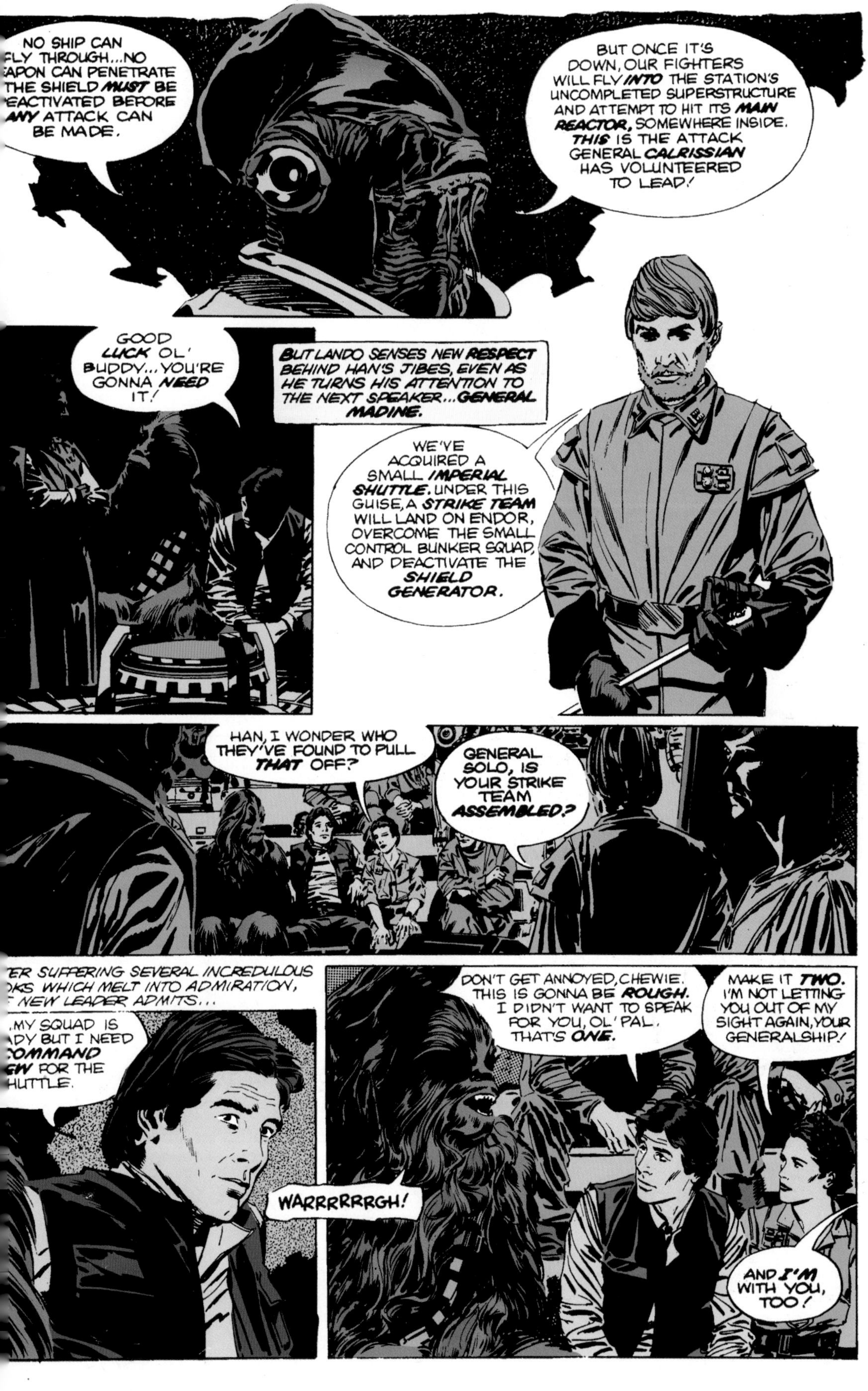
NO SHIP CAN FLY THROUGH... NO EAPON CAN PENETRATE THE SHIELD MUST BE EACTIVATED BEFORE ANY ATTACK CAN BE MADE.
BUT ONCE IT'S DOWN, OUR FIGHTERS WILL FLY INTO THE STATION'S UNCOMPLETED SUPERSTRUCTURE AND ATTEMPT TO HIT ITS MAIN REACTOR, SOMEWHERE INSIDE. THIS IS THE ATTACK GENERAL CALRISSIAN HAS VOLUNTEERED TO LEAD!
GOOD LUCK OL' BUDDY... YOU'RE GONNA NEED IT!
BUT LANDO SENSES NEW RESPECT BEHIND HAN'S JIBES, EVEN AS HE TURNS HIS ATTENTION TO THE NEXT SPEAKER... GENERAL MADINE.
WE'VE ACQUIRED A SMALL IMPERIAL SHUTTLE. UNDER THIS GUISE, A STRIKE TEAM WILL LAND ON ENDOR, OVERCOME THE SMALL CONTROL BUNKER SQUAD, AND DEACTIVATE THE SHIELD GENERATOR.
HAN, I WONDER WHO THEY'VE FOUND TO PULL THAT OFF?
GENERAL SOLO, IS YOUR STRIKE TEAM ASSEMBLED?
ER SUFFERING SEVERAL INCREDULOUS OKS WHICH MELT INTO ADMIRATION, NEW LEADER ADMITS...
MY SQUAD IS ADY BUT I NEED COMMAND EW FOR THE HUTTLE.
WARRRRRRGH!
DON'T GET ANNOYED, CHEWIE. THIS IS GONNA BE ROUGH. I DIDN'T WANT TO SPEAK FOR YOU, OL' PAL. THAT'S ONE.
MAKE IT TWO. I'M NOT LETTING YOU OUT OF MY SIGHT AGAIN, YOUR GENERALSHIP!
AND I'M WITH YOU, TOO!

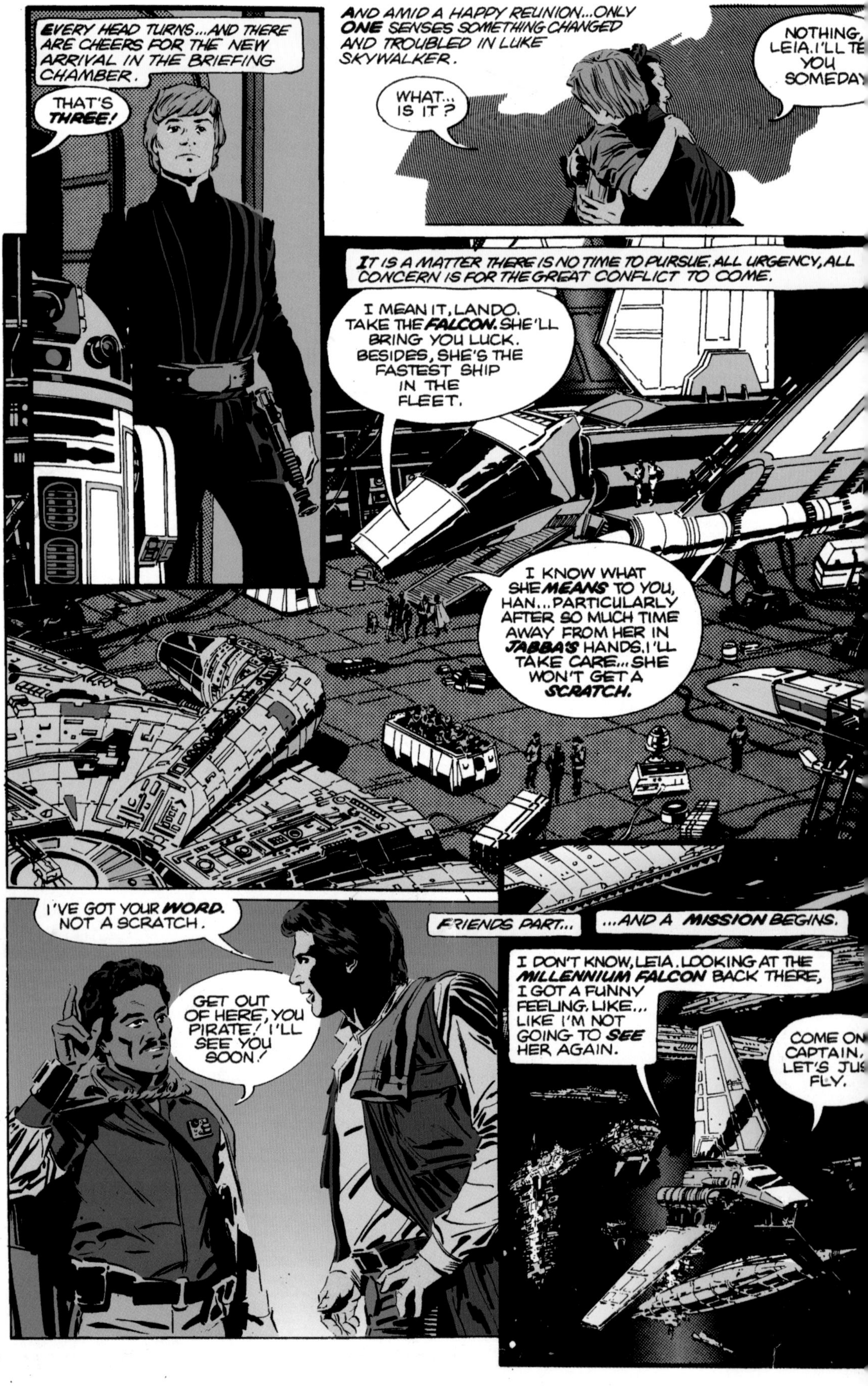
EVERY HEAD TURNS...AND THERE ARE CHEERS FOR THE NEW ARRIVAL IN THE BRIEFING CHAMBER.
THAT'S THREE!
AND AMID A HAPPY REUNION...ONLY ONE SENSES SOMETHING CHANGED AND TROUBLED IN LUKE SKYWALKER.
WHAT... IS IT?
NOTHING, LEIA. I'LL TE YOU SOMEDAY
IT IS A MATTER THERE IS NO TIME TO PURSUE. ALL URGENCY, ALL CONCERN IS FOR THE GREAT CONFLICT TO COME.
I MEAN IT, LANDO. TAKE THE FALCON. SHE'LL BRING YOU LUCK. BESIDES, SHE'S THE FASTEST SHIP IN THE FLEET.
I KNOW WHAT SHE MEANS TO YOU, HAN... PARTICULARLY AFTER SO MUCH TIME AWAY FROM HER IN JABBA'S HANDS. I'LL TAKE CARE... SHE WON'T GET A SCRATCH.
I'VE GOT YOUR WORD. NOT A SCRATCH.
GET OUT OF HERE, YOU PIRATE! I'LL SEE YOU SOON!
FRIENDS PART...
...AND A MISSION BEGINS.
I DON'T KNOW, LEIA. LOOKING AT THE MILLENNIUM FALCON BACK THERE, I GOT A FUNNY FEELING. LIKE... LIKE I'M NOT GOING TO SEE HER AGAIN.
COME ON CAPTAIN, LET'S JUS FLY.

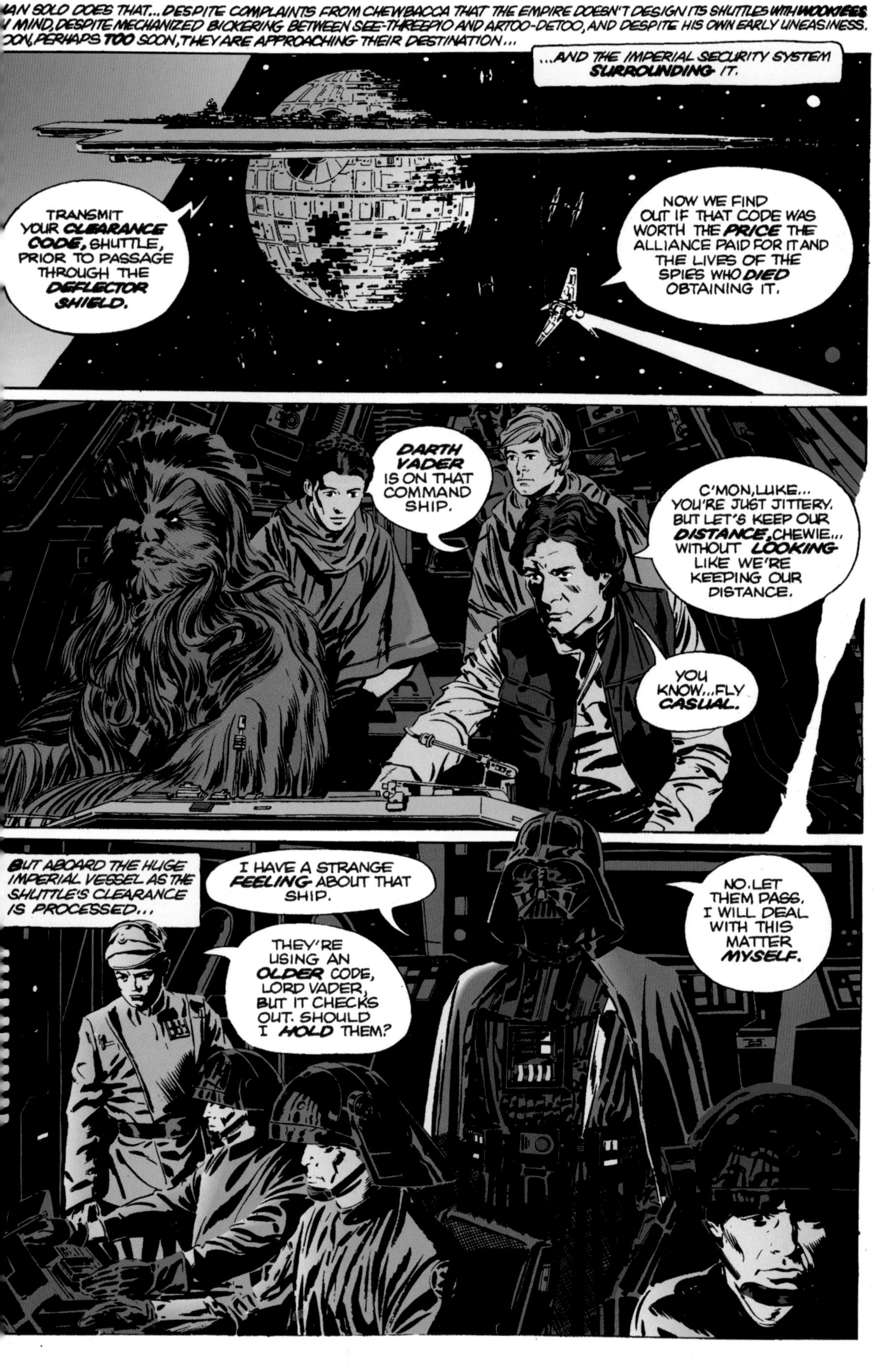
AN SOLO DOES THAT... DESPITE COMPLAINTS FROM CHEWBACCA THAT THE EMPIRE DOESN'T DESIGN ITS SHUTTLES WITH WOOKIEES N MIND, DESPITE MECHANIZED BICKERING BETWEEN SEE-THREEPIO AND ARTOO-DETOO, AND DESPITE HIS OWN EARLY UNEASINESS. OON, PERHAPS TOO SOON, THEY ARE APPROACHING THEIR DESTINATION...
...AND THE IMPERIAL SECURITY SYSTEM SURROUNDING IT.
TRANSMIT YOUR CLEARANCE CODE, SHUTTLE, PRIOR TO PASSAGE THROUGH THE DEFLECTOR SHIELD.
NOW WE FIND OUT IF THAT CODE WAS WORTH THE PRICE THE ALLIANCE PAID FOR IT AND THE LIVES OF THE SPIES WHO DIED OBTAINING IT.
DARTH VADER IS ON THAT COMMAND SHIP.
C'MON, LUKE... YOU'RE JUST JITTERY. BUT LET'S KEEP OUR DISTANCE, CHEWIE... WITHOUT LOOKING LIKE WE'RE KEEPING OUR DISTANCE.
YOU KNOW...FLY CASUAL.
BUT ABOARD THE HUGE IMPERIAL VESSEL AS THE SHUTTLE'S CLEARANCE IS PROCESSED...
I HAVE A STRANGE FEELING ABOUT THAT SHIP.
THEY'RE USING AN OLDER CODE, LORD VADER, BUT IT CHECKS OUT. SHOULD I HOLD THEM?
NO. LET THEM PASS. I WILL DEAL WITH THIS MATTER MYSELF.

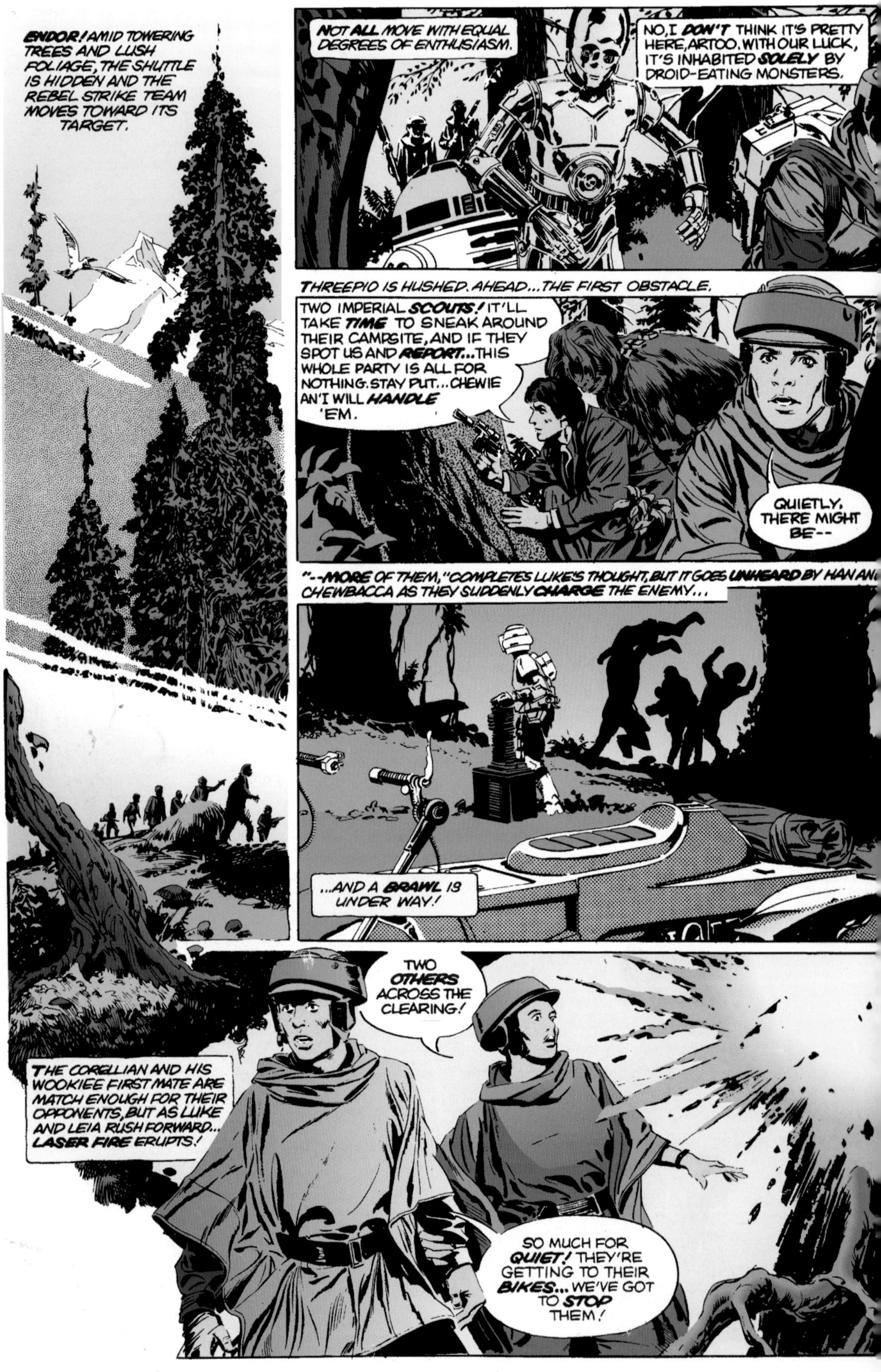
ENDOR! AMID TOWERING TREES AND LUSH FOLIAGE, THE SHUTTLE IS HIDDEN AND THE REBEL STRIKE TEAM MOVES TOWARD ITS TARGET.
NOT ALL MOVE WITH EQUAL DEGREES OF ENTHUSIASM.
NO, I DON'T THINK IT'S PRETTY HERE, ARTOO. WITH OUR LUCK, IT'S INHABITED SOLELY BY DROID-EATING MONSTERS.
THREEPIO IS HUSHED. AHEAD... THE FIRST OBSTACLE.
TWO IMPERIAL SCOUTS! IT'LL TAKE TIME TO SNEAK AROUND THEIR CAMPSITE, AND IF THEY SPOT US AND REPORT... THIS WHOLE PARTY IS ALL FOR NOTHING. STAY PUT... CHEWIE AN' I WILL HANDLE 'EM.
QUIETLY. THERE MIGHT BE--
"--MORE OF THEM," COMPLETES LUKE'S THOUGHT, BUT IT GOES UNHEARD BY HAN AN
CHEWBACCA AS THEY SUDDENLY CHARGE THE ENEMY...
...AND A BRAWL IS UNDER WAY!
THE CORELLIAN AND HIS WOOKIEE FIRST MATE ARE MATCH ENOUGH FOR THEIR OPPONENTS, BUT AS LUKE AND LEIA RUSH FORWARD... LASER FIRE ERUPTS!
TWO OTHERS ACROSS THE CLEARING!
SO MUCH FOR QUIET! THEY'RE GETTING TO THEIR BIKES... WE'VE GOT TO STOP THEM!

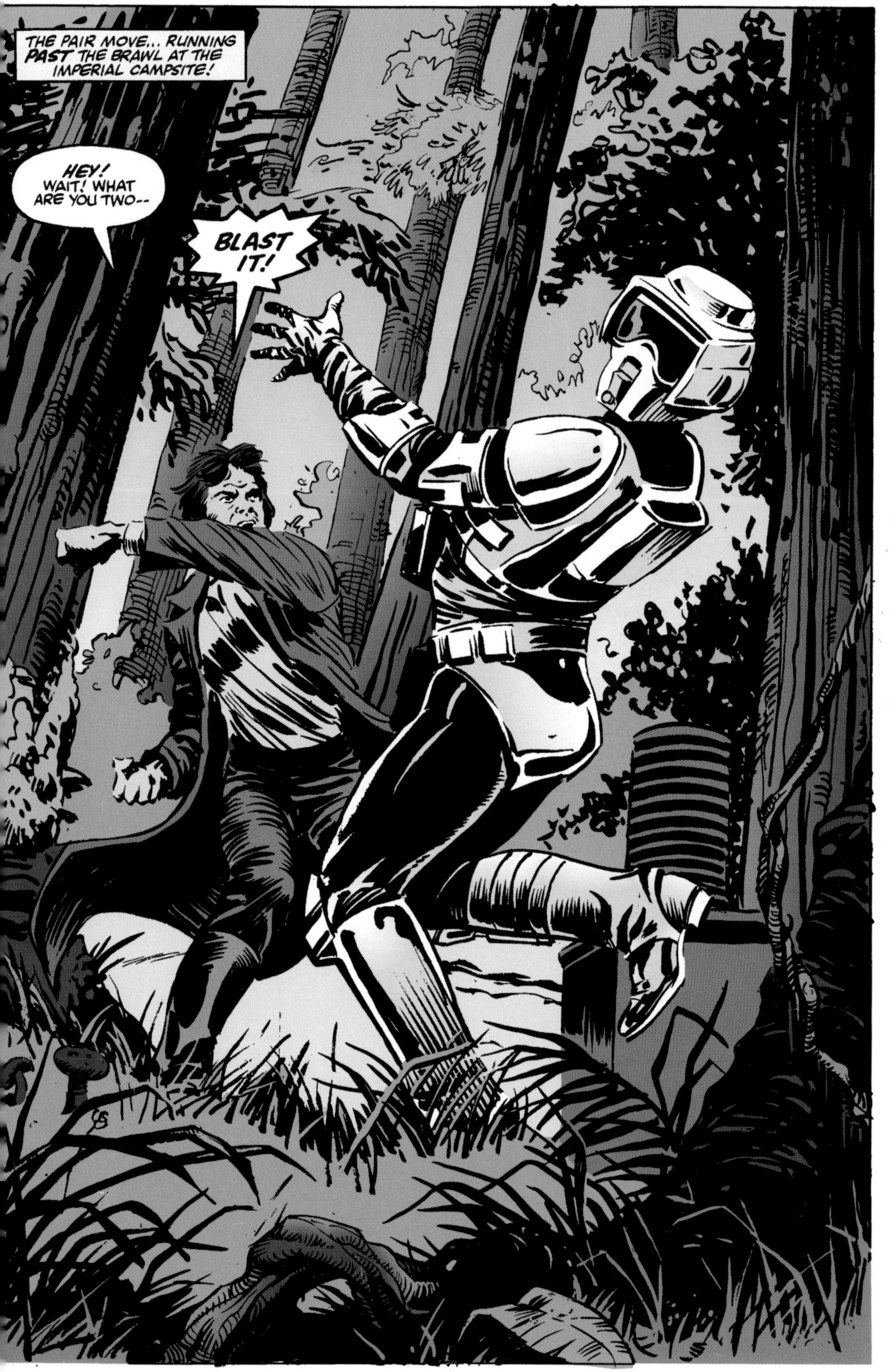
THE PAIR MOVE... RUNNING PAST THE BRAWL AT THE IMPERIAL CAMPSITE!
HEY! WAIT! WHAT ARE YOU TWO--
BLAST IT!

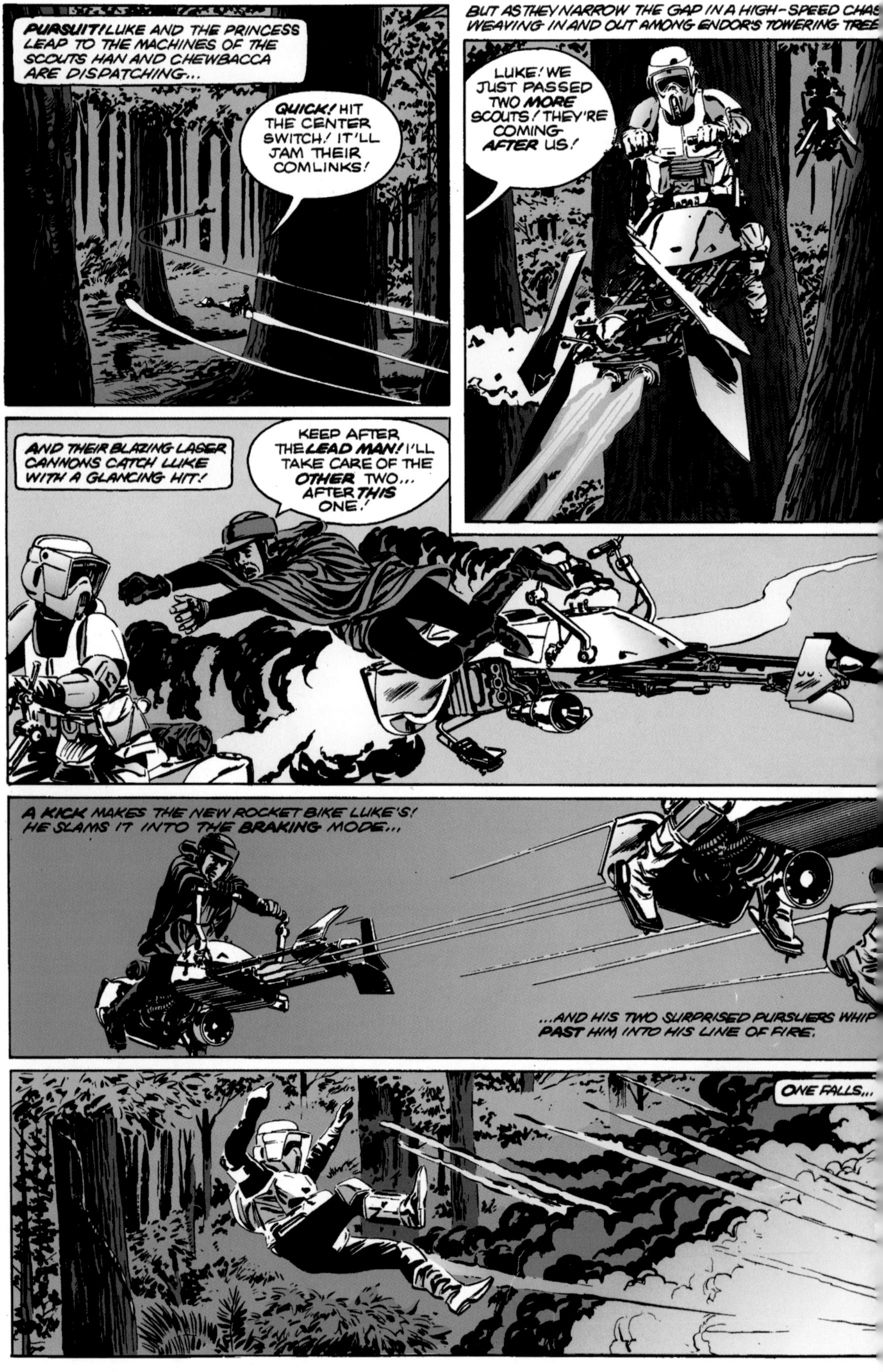
PURSUIT! LUKE AND THE PRINCESS LEAP TO THE MACHINES OF THE SCOUTS HAN AND CHEWBACCA ARE DISPATCHING...
QUICK! HIT THE CENTER SWITCH! IT'LL JAM THEIR COMLINKS!
BUT AS THEY NARROW THE GAP IN A HIGH-SPEED CHAS WEAVING IN AND OUT AMONG ENDOR'S TOWERING TREE
LUKE! WE JUST PASSED TWO MORE SCOUTS! THEY'RE COMING AFTER US!
AND THEIR BLAZING LASER CANNONS CATCH LUKE WITH A GLANCING HIT!
KEEP AFTER THE LEAD MAN! I'LL TAKE CARE OF THE OTHER TWO... AFTER THIS ONE!
A KICK MAKES THE NEW ROCKET BIKE LUKE'S! HE SLAMS IT INTO THE BRAKING MODE...
...AND HIS TWO SURPRISED PURSUIERS WHIP PAST HIM INTO HIS LINE OF FIRE.
ONE FALLS...

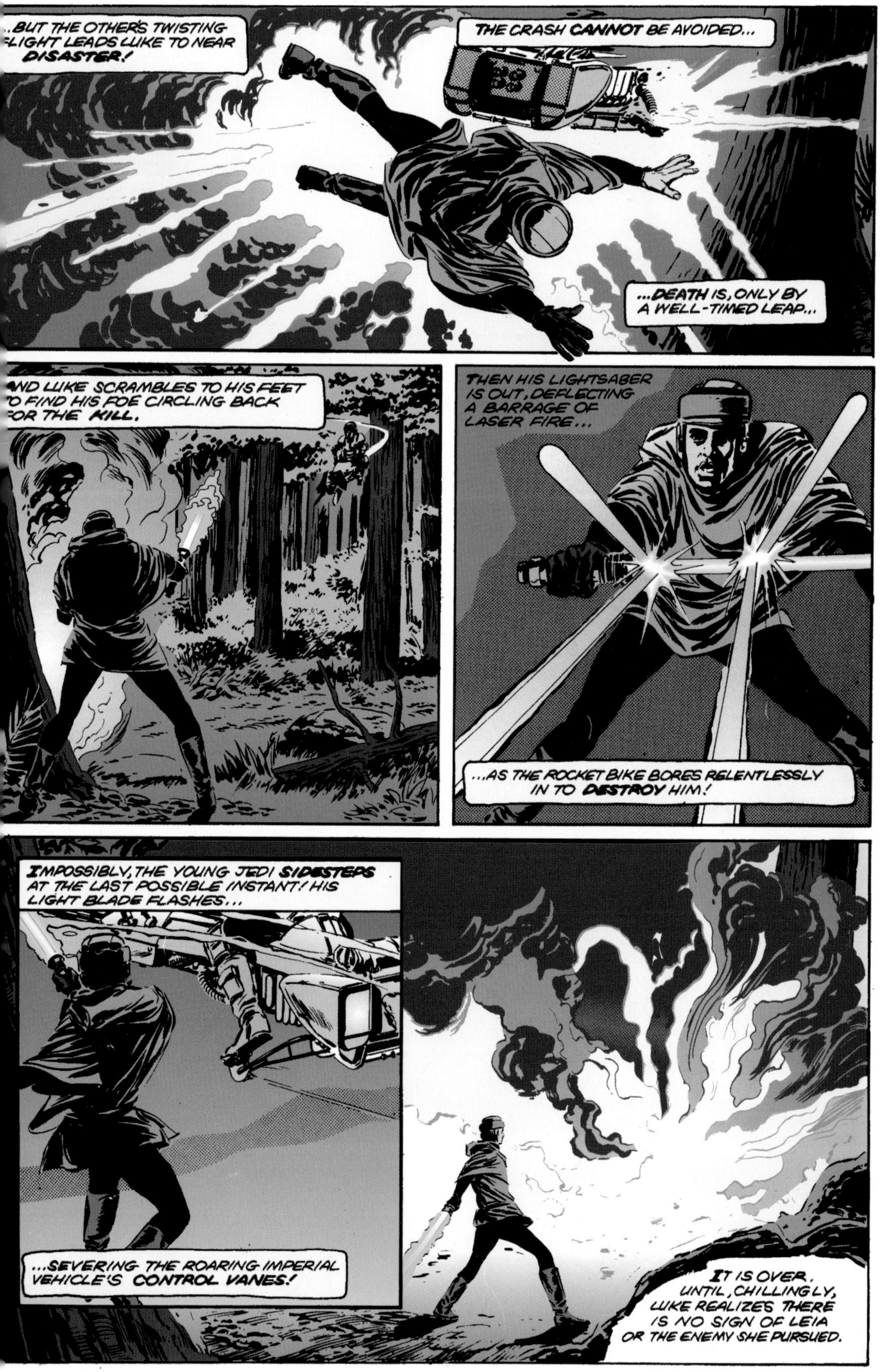
..BUT THE OTHER'S TWISTING FLIGHT LEADS LUKE TO NEAR DISASTER!
THE CRASH CANNOT BE AVOIDED...
...DEATH IS, ONLY BY A WELL-TIMED LEAP...
AND LUKE SCRAMBLES TO HIS FEET TO FIND HIS FOE CIRCLING BACK FOR THE KILL.
THEN HIS LIGHTSABER IS OUT, DEFLECTING A BARRAGE OF LASER FIRE...
...AS THE ROCKET BIKE BORES RELENTLESSLY IN TO DESTROY HIM!
IMPOSSIBLY, THE YOUNG JEDI SIDESTEPS AT THE LAST POSSIBLE INSTANT! HIS LIGHT BLADE FLASHES...
...SEVERING THE ROARING IMPERIAL VEHICLE'S CONTROL VANES!
IT IS OVER. UNTIL, CHILLINGLY, LUKE REALIZES THERE IS NO SIGN OF LEIA OR THE ENEMY SHE PURSUED.

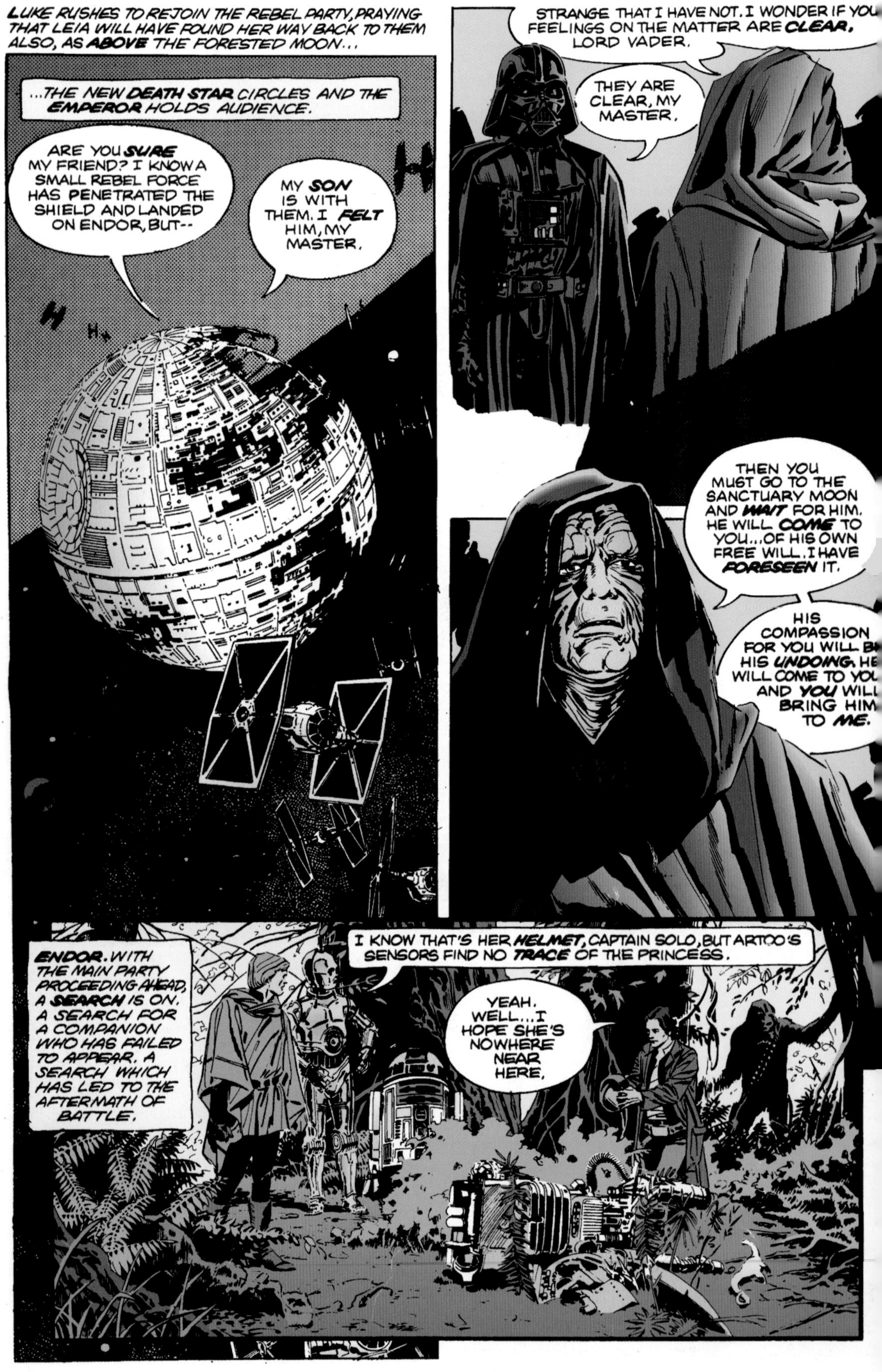
LUKE RUSHES TO REJOIN THE REBEL PARTY, PRAYING THAT LEIA WILL HAVE FOUND HER WAY BACK TO THEM ALSO, AS ABOVE THE FORESTED MOON...
...THE NEW DEATH STAR CIRCLES AND THE EMPEROR HOLDS AUDIENCE.
ARE YOU SURE MY FRIEND? I KNOW A SMALL REBEL FORCE HAS PENETRATED THE SHIELD AND LANDED ON ENDOR, BUT--
MY SON IS WITH THEM. I FELT HIM, MY MASTER.
STRANGE THAT I HAVE NOT. I WONDER IF YOU FEELINGS ON THE MATTER ARE CLEAR, LORD VADER.
THEY ARE CLEAR, MY MASTER.
THEN YOU MUST GO TO THE SANCTUARY MOON AND WAIT FOR HIM. HE WILL COME TO YOU...OF HIS OWN FREE WILL. I HAVE FORESEEN IT.
HIS COMPASSION FOR YOU WILL B HIS UNDOING. HE WILL COME TO YOU AND YOU WILL BRING HIM TO ME.
ENDOR. WITH THE MAIN PARTY PROCEEDING AHEAD, A SEARCH IS ON. A SEARCH FOR A COMPANION WHO HAS FAILED TO APPEAR. A SEARCH WHICH HAS LED TO THE AFTERMATH OF BATTLE.
I KNOW THAT'S HER HELMET, CAPTAIN SOLO, BUT ARTOO'S SENSORS FIND NO TRACE OF THE PRINCESS.
YEAH. WELL...I HOPE SHE'S NOWHERE NEAR HERE.

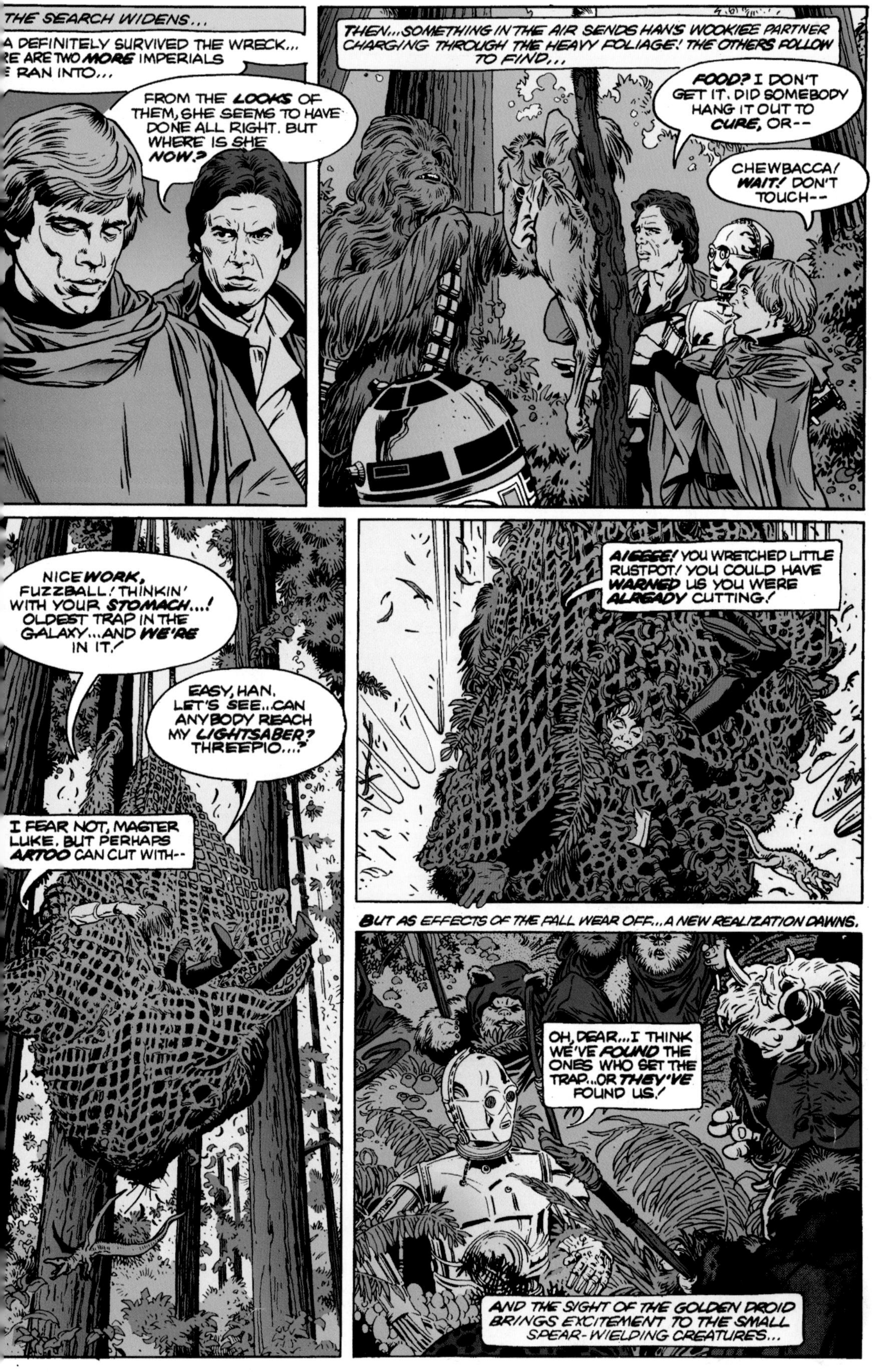
THE SEARCH WIDENS...
A DEFINITELY SURVIVED THE WRECK... RE ARE TWO MORE IMPERIALS E RAN INTO...
FROM THE LOOKS OF THEM, SHE SEEMS TO HAVE DONE ALL RIGHT. BUT WHERE IS SHE NOW?
THEN...SOMETHING IN THE AIR SENDS HAN'S WOOKIEE PARTNER CHARGING THROUGH THE HEAVY FOLIAGE! THE OTHERS FOLLOW TO FIND...
FOOD? I DON'T GET IT. DID SOMEBODY HANG IT OUT TO CURE, OR--
CHEWBACCA! WAIT! DON'T TOUCH--
NICE WORK, FUZZBALL! THINKIN' WITH YOUR STOMACH...! OLDEST TRAP IN THE GALAXY...AND WE'RE IN IT!
EASY, HAN. LET'S SEE...CAN ANYBODY REACH MY LIGHTSABER? THREEPIO...?
I FEAR NOT, MASTER LUKE. BUT PERHAPS ARTOO CAN CUT WITH--
AIEEEE! YOU WRETCHED LITTLE RUSTPOT! YOU COULD HAVE WARNED US YOU WERE ALREADY CUTTING!
BUT AS EFFECTS OF THE FALL WEAR OFF...A NEW REALIZATION DAWNS.
OH, DEAR...I THINK WE'VE FOUND THE ONES WHO SET THE TRAP...OR THEY'VE FOUND US!
AND THE SIGHT OF THE GOLDEN DROID BRINGS EXCITEMENT TO THE SMALL SPEAR-WIELDING CREATURES...

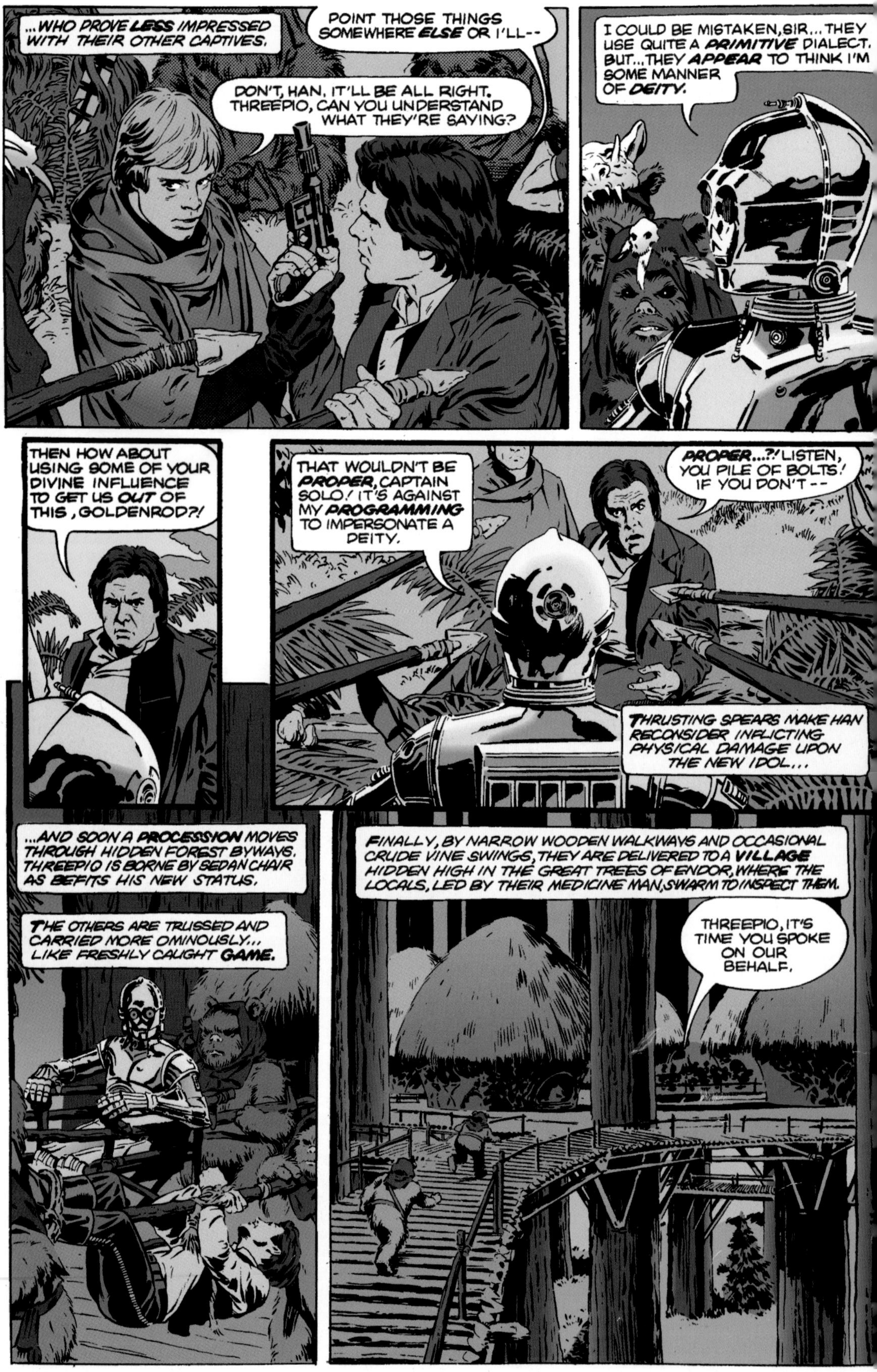

...WHO PROVE LESS IMPRESSED WITH THEIR OTHER CAPTIVES.
POINT THOSE THINGS SOMEWHERE ELSE OR I'LL--
DON'T, HAN. IT'LL BE ALL RIGHT. THREEPIO, CAN YOU UNDERSTAND WHAT THEY'RE SAYING?
I COULD BE MISTAKEN, SIR... THEY USE QUITE A PRIMITIVE DIALECT. BUT...THEY APPEAR TO THINK I'M SOME MANNER OF DEITY.
THEN HOW ABOUT USING SOME OF YOUR DIVINE INFLUENCE TO GET US OUT OF THIS, GOLDENROD?!
THAT WOULDN'T BE PROPER, CAPTAIN SOLO! IT'S AGAINST MY PROGRAMMING TO IMPERSONATE A DEITY.
PROPER...?! LISTEN, YOU PILE OF BOLTS! IF YOU DON'T --
THRUSTING SPEARS MAKE HAN RECONSIDER INFLICTING PHYSICAL DAMAGE UPON THE NEW IDOL...
...AND SOON A PROCESSION MOVES THROUGH HIDDEN FOREST BYWAYS. THREEPIO IS BORNE BY SEDAN CHAIR AS BEFITS HIS NEW STATUS.
THE OTHERS ARE TRUSSED AND CARRIED MORE OMINOUSLY... LIKE FRESHLY CAUGHT GAME.
FINALLY, BY NARROW WOODEN WALKWAYS AND OCCASIONAL CRUDE VINE SWINGS, THEY ARE DELIVERED TO A VILLAGE HIDDEN HIGH IN THE GREAT TREES OF ENDOR, WHERE THE LOCALS, LED BY THEIR MEDICINE MAN, SWARM TO INSPECT THEM.
THREEPIO, IT'S TIME YOU SPOKE ON OUR BEHALF.

THE RESULTS ARE NOT ENCOURAGING. FIREWOOD IS STACKED UNDER HAN SOLO.

WELL? WHAT DID THEY SAY?

I'M RATHER EMBARRASSED, CAPTAIN. IT APPEARS **YOU** ARE TO BE THE **MAIN COURSE** AT A BANQUET IN **MY** HONOR. THE MEDICINE MAN IS QUITE OFFENDED I SHOULD SUGGEST OTHERWISE.

LOOK, BRIGHT EYES, YOU'D BETTER **TELL** THAT SAWED-OFF LITTLE --

...LL THEM YOU ARE ALL ...Y FRIENDS, THREEPIO... ...AND MUST BE SET FREE!

LEIA! H-HOW...?

ONE OF THESE LITTLE FOLK-- THE **EWOKS**--FOUND ME AFTER MY **RUN-IN** WITH THE IMPERIALS. I GUESS HE WAS **IMPRESSED** SINCE THE EWOKS DON'T LIKE THEM EITHER!

BUT SHARING MUTUAL ENEMIES IS NOT ENOUGH TO DISSUADE THE MEDICINE MAN FROM HONORING THE TRIBE'S NEW DEITY.

THREEPIO, TELL THEM IF THEY DON'T DO AS YOU WISH, YOU'LL BECOME **ANGRY** AND USE YOUR **MAGIC.**

SIR...? **WHAT** MAGIC? I COULDN'T --

...TELL THEM.

I-I AM MASTER LUKE, BUT THEY DON'T **BELIEVE** ME, SIR, JUST AS I TOLD YOU--

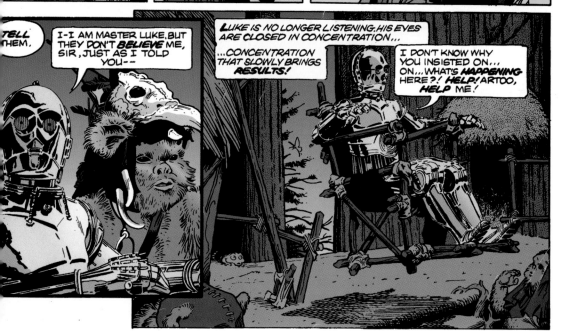

LUKE IS NO LONGER LISTENING. HIS EYES ARE CLOSED IN CONCENTRATION...

...CONCENTRATION THAT SLOWLY BRINGS **RESULTS!**

I DON'T KNOW WHY YOU INSISTED ON... ON... WHAT'S **HAPPENING** HERE?! **HELP!** ARTOO, **HELP** ME!

GENTLY, THE EWOK DEITY IS LOWERED BACK TO THE GROUND. SUDDENLY, THERE IS A RUSH TO FREE HIS FRIENDS.

THANKS, THREEPIO!

WHY... WHY, I DIDN'T KNOW I HAD IT *IN* ME, MASTER LUKE!

A MEETING FOLLOWS IN THE TRIBAL CHIEFTAIN'S HUT WHERE THE PURPOSE OF THE REBEL MISSION AGAINST THE EMPIRE IS MADE CLEAR BY THREEPIO...

...OR AT LEAST AS CLEAR AS THE DROID'S IMITATION OF THE SQUEAKY EWOK DIALECT, WITH OCCASIONAL SOUND EFFECTS THROWN IN, CAN MAKE A SHORT HISTORY OF THE GALACTIC CIVIL WAR.

AND MANY ARGUMENTS, DISCUSSIONS, AND SPEECHES LATER...

WE ARE NOW PART OF THE *TRIBE*, CAPTAIN. THE CHIEF HAS VOWED TO HELP US IN ANY WAY TO RID THEIR LAND OF THE EVIL ONES.

JUST WHAT I'VE ALWAYS WANTED! WELL... *SHORT* HELP IS BETTER THAN *NO* HELP!

BUT NOT EVERYONE IS QUITE SO FORGIVING OVER THE INDIGNITIES SUFFERED.

BRAAAAP!

STILL, THE MEETING IN THE HUT IN TIME BECOMES A CELEBRATION. AS THE REVELRY GROWS, LUKE SKYWALKER MOVES QUIETLY AWAY INTO THE STILLNESS OUTSIDE, BUT HIS DEPARTURE DOES NOT GO UNNOTICED.

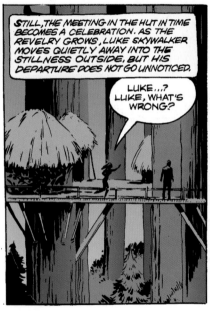

LUKE...? LUKE, WHAT'S WRONG?

EVERYTHING, I'M AFRAID, OR NOTHING. MAYBE THINGS ARE FINALLY GOING TO BE THE WAY THEY WERE *MEANT* TO BE.

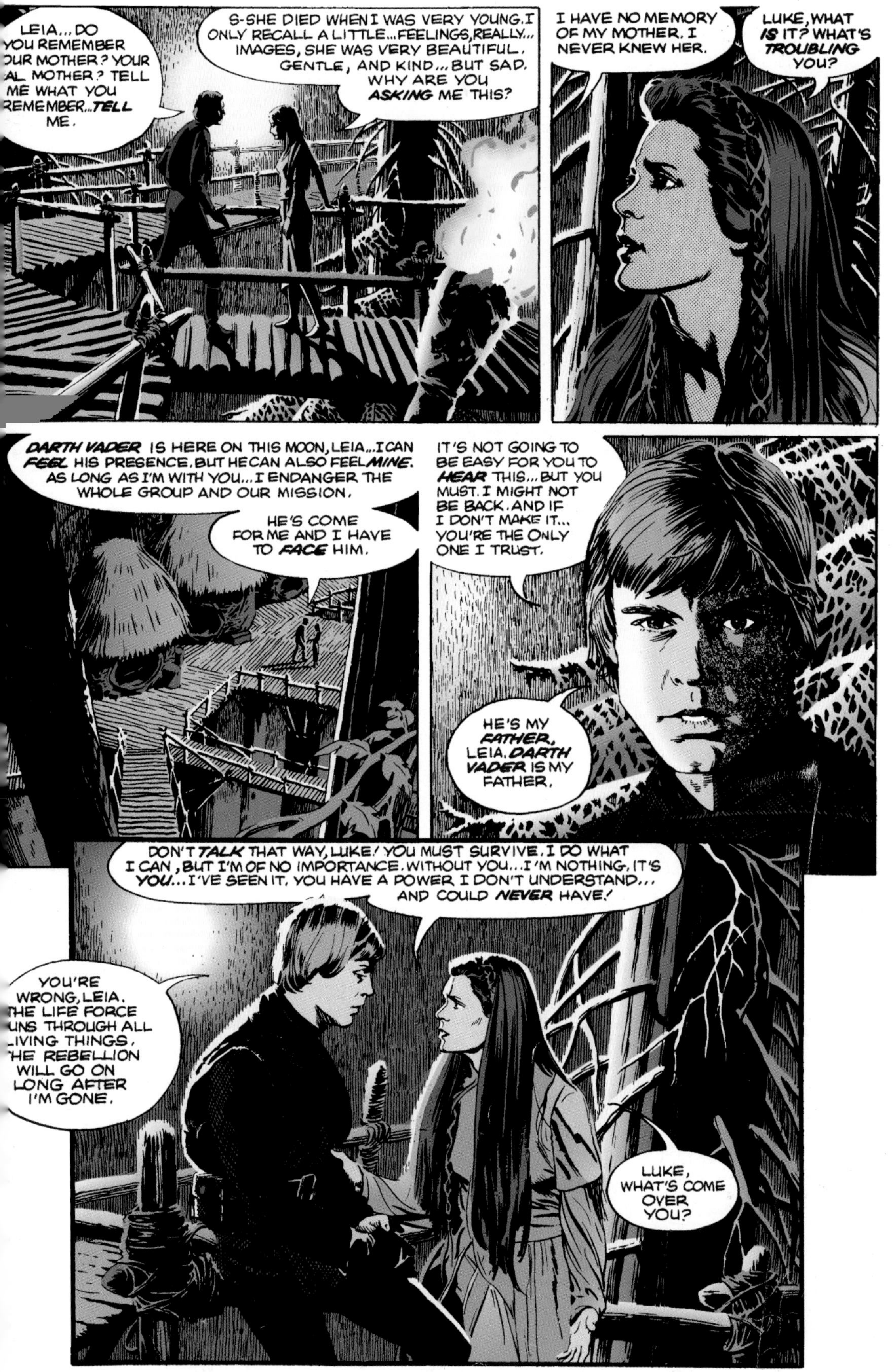
LEIA... DO YOU REMEMBER OUR MOTHER? YOUR AL MOTHER? TELL ME WHAT YOU REMEMBER... TELL ME.
S-SHE DIED WHEN I WAS VERY YOUNG. I ONLY RECALL A LITTLE... FEELINGS, REALLY... IMAGES, SHE WAS VERY BEAUTIFUL. GENTLE, AND KIND... BUT SAD. WHY ARE YOU ASKING ME THIS?
I HAVE NO MEMORY OF MY MOTHER. I NEVER KNEW HER.
LUKE, WHAT IS IT? WHAT'S TROUBLING YOU?
DARTH VADER IS HERE ON THIS MOON, LEIA... I CAN FEEL HIS PRESENCE. BUT HE CAN ALSO FEEL MINE. AS LONG AS I'M WITH YOU... I ENDANGER THE WHOLE GROUP AND OUR MISSION.
HE'S COME FOR ME AND I HAVE TO FACE HIM.
IT'S NOT GOING TO BE EASY FOR YOU TO HEAR THIS... BUT YOU MUST. I MIGHT NOT BE BACK. AND IF I DON'T MAKE IT... YOU'RE THE ONLY ONE I TRUST.
HE'S MY FATHER, LEIA. DARTH VADER IS MY FATHER.
DON'T TALK THAT WAY, LUKE! YOU MUST SURVIVE. I DO WHAT I CAN, BUT I'M OF NO IMPORTANCE. WITHOUT YOU... I'M NOTHING. IT'S YOU... I'VE SEEN IT. YOU HAVE A POWER I DON'T UNDERSTAND... AND COULD NEVER HAVE!
YOU'RE WRONG, LEIA. HE LIFE FORCE UNS THROUGH ALL IVING THINGS. HE REBELLION WILL GO ON LONG AFTER I'M GONE.
LUKE, WHAT'S COME OVER YOU?

THE FORCE IS **STRONG** IN MY FAMILY, LEIA. MY FATHER HAS IT. I HAVE IT. AND MY **SISTER** HAS IT... **YOU**, LEIA! BELIEVE ME... AND BELIEVE I **MUST** GO TO DARTH VADER. I'M THE ONLY ONE WHO CAN **SAVE** HIM.

RUN AWAY, LUKE,... **FAR** AWAY! IF HE CAN FEEL YOUR PRESENCE, GO **AWAY** FROM THIS PLACE! I WISH I COULD GO **WITH** YOU!

NO, YOU DON'T. YOU'VE NEVER FALTERED, LEI WHEN HAN AND I AND OTHERS DOUBTED, YOU'VE ALWAYS BEE STRONG... NEVER TURNED AW FROM YOUR RESPONSIBILIT I CAN'T SAY THE SAME.

WELL, NOW WE'RE **BOTH** GOING TO FULFIL OUR DESTIN

*READING LUKE'S UNWAVERING EYES, LEIA **KNOWS** SHE HAS HEARD THE TRUTH.*

LUKE, **WHY?** WHY MUST YOU CONFRONT HIM?

THERE'S **GOOD** IN HIM. I'VE FELT IT. HE WON'T TURN ME OVER TO THE EMPEROR. I CAN TURN HIM BACK TO THE GOOD SIDE. I MUST **TRY**, LEIA. HE'S OUR FATHER.

TEARS GLISTEN IN THE EYES OF THE PRINCESS, BUT SHE SEN THERE IS NOTHING MORE TO BE SAID. GENTLY, LUKE SKYWALKE EMBRACES HER...

GOOD BYE, SWEET, SWEET LEIA.

THEN HE MOVES AWAY, DISAPPEARING INTO THE MIST AND THE NIGHT.

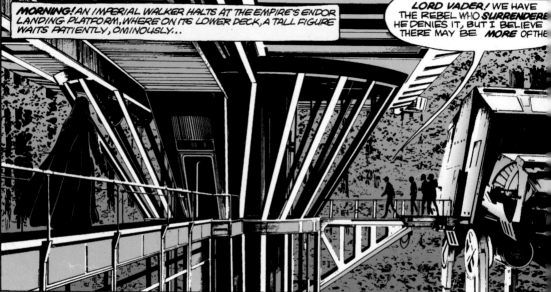

MORNING! AN IMPERIAL WALKER HALTS AT THE EMPIRE'S ENDOR LANDING PLATFORM, WHERE ON ITS LOWER DECK, A TALL FIGURE WAITS PATIENTLY, OMINOUSLY...

LORD VADER! WE HAVE THE REBEL WHO **SURRENDERE** HE DENIES IT, BUT I BELIEVE THERE MAY BE **MORE** OF THE

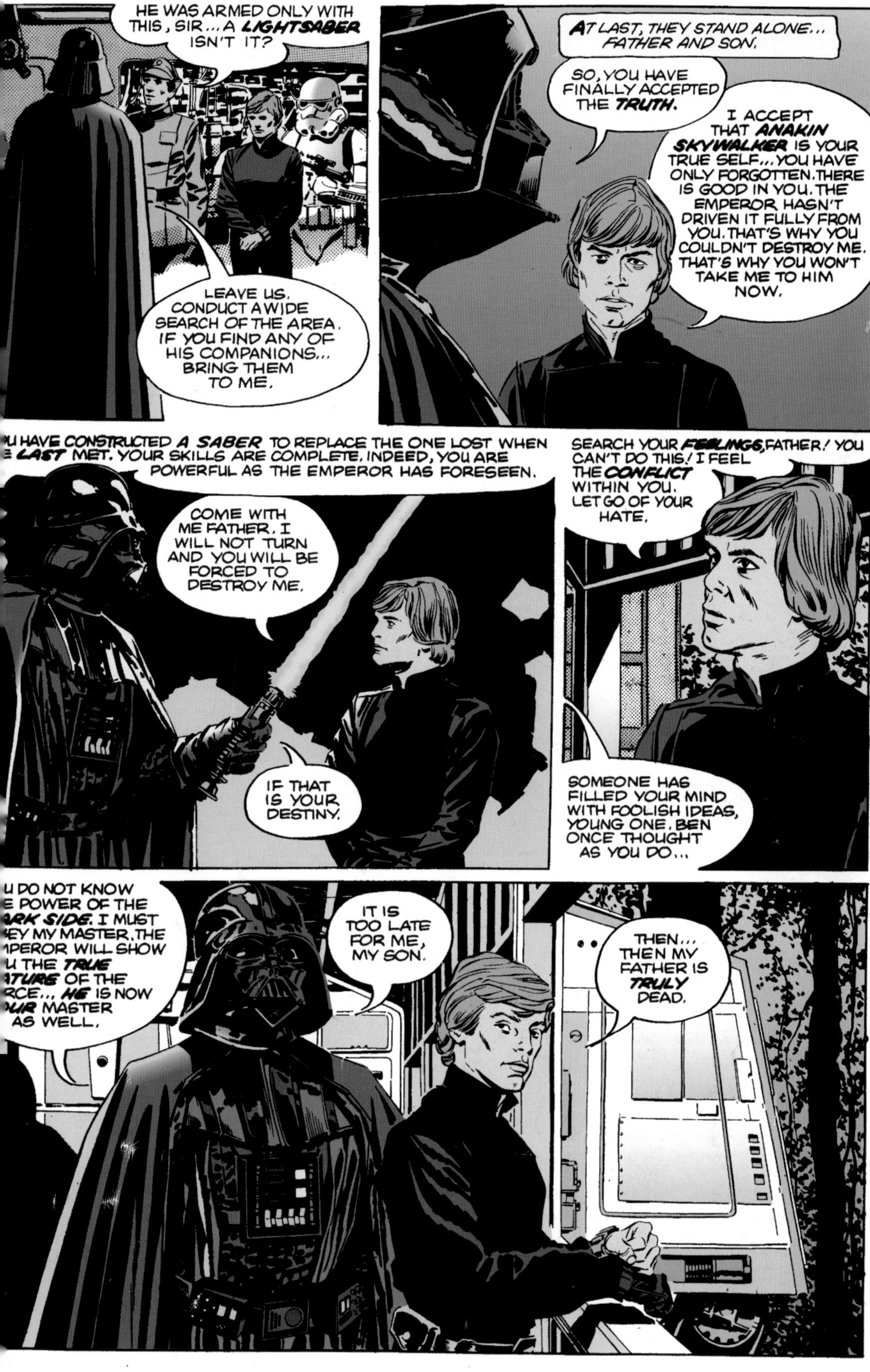

HE WAS ARMED ONLY WITH THIS, SIR... A LIGHTSABER ISN'T IT?
LEAVE US. CONDUCT A WIDE SEARCH OF THE AREA. IF YOU FIND ANY OF HIS COMPANIONS... BRING THEM TO ME.
AT LAST, THEY STAND ALONE... FATHER AND SON.
SO, YOU HAVE FINALLY ACCEPTED THE TRUTH.
I ACCEPT THAT ANAKIN SKYWALKER IS YOUR TRUE SELF... YOU HAVE ONLY FORGOTTEN. THERE IS GOOD IN YOU. THE EMPEROR HASN'T DRIVEN IT FULLY FROM YOU. THAT'S WHY YOU COULDN'T DESTROY ME. THAT'S WHY YOU WON'T TAKE ME TO HIM NOW.
U HAVE CONSTRUCTED A SABER TO REPLACE THE ONE LOST WHEN E LAST MET. YOUR SKILLS ARE COMPLETE. INDEED, YOU ARE POWERFUL AS THE EMPEROR HAS FORESEEN.
COME WITH ME FATHER. I WILL NOT TURN AND YOU WILL BE FORCED TO DESTROY ME.
IF THAT IS YOUR DESTINY.
SEARCH YOUR FEELINGS, FATHER! YOU CAN'T DO THIS! I FEEL THE CONFLICT WITHIN YOU. LET GO OF YOUR HATE.
SOMEONE HAS FILLED YOUR MIND WITH FOOLISH IDEAS, YOUNG ONE. BEN ONCE THOUGHT AS YOU DO...
U DO NOT KNOW E POWER OF THE ARK SIDE. I MUST EY MY MASTER. THE MPEROR WILL SHOW U THE TRUE ATURE OF THE RCE... HE IS NOW UR MASTER AS WELL.
IT IS TOO LATE FOR ME, MY SON.
THEN... THEN MY FATHER IS TRULY DEAD.